THIS BOOK BELONGS TO:

OTHER MY FRIEND PARIS BOOKS

Published by:

New Year Publishing, LLC 144 Diablo Ranch Ct. Danville, CA 94506 USA

orders@newyearpublishing.com http://www.newyearpublishing.com

Library of Congress Control Number: 2007930313
ISBN: 978-0976009559

To my cousins Jenna and Sarah who taught me how to be a great Big Sister.

My name is Paris.
I am three years
old and I live near
San Francisco,
California with my
Mommy and Daddy.

Things are about to change around here. I'm very excited. Are you, Dolly?

Yesterday my Mommy had my twin sisters.
It's the same hospital where I was born.

Grandma was reading me a book in the waiting room when Daddy came in to tell us that they were born and that they are named Liberty and Victoria. He was very happy.

I can't wait to share
my Blankie with them!

They are very small and Daddy told me that they would stay in their own special room in the hospital.

congrats

IT'S TWO GIRLS
I only saw Mommy for a few minutes because she was very tired.

I got to spend that night at Grandma and Grandpa's house.

The next day Grandma and I went back to the hospital and I got to look at my twins through the nursery window. I think that Liberty smiled at me.

Lots of people keep coming to the hospital to see my Mommy and look at my sisters through the glass. Sometimes they bring me presents.

The Doctor told me that my sisters are growing nicely and that I should be a good girl for Mommy and Daddy.

When my other Grandma comes over, she always spends time with me before she visits my sisters.

Our neighbors put up two big storks in our yard to announce the arrival of my sisters.

Mommy finally came home today.
Daddy and I are taking care of her.

Daddy made me macaroni and cheese for dinner tonight. It's not as good as Mommy's but he tried hard.

My twins came home today!
I finally got to give them my
special Blankie.

CPSIA information can be obtained
at www.ICGtesting.com
Printed in the USA
437513LV00006B/15

* 9 7 8 0 9 7 6 0 0 9 5 5 9 *